the monster

the monster

by
Peter Kray

The Monster
By Peter Kray

www.turnthelightonthemonster.com

Library of Congress Catalog-in-Publication Data: 2003090129

ISBN, Print ed. 0-9715715-1-1

First Printing 2003, Printed in U.S.A.

Copyright 2003, The Coghill Foundation, Inc.
4223 South Bellaire Circle, Englewood, CO 80110

Contents

foreword

This book can change your life. It was written to help you be healthier, happier and more informed about your body and all of your health decisions. No matter who you are. No matter what you do. No matter where in the world you live.

At its core, The Monster is the result of three simple questions: What do you consider good for your health? What do you consider bad for your health? And, what do you consider good medicine? Over a two-year span, those questions were posed to everyone from medical doctors to witch doctors, nutritionists to nurses, psychologists to poets and scientists to ski bums. The questions were asked of people who were chronically and even critically ill, and people who could barely remember having more than a cold in their lifetimes. The Monster is the compilation of countless hours of inquiry and the answers received in response to those three questions.

No miracle cure, diet or fitness plan awaits in the following pages. The Monster is an allegory about rational thought and how it applies to your health, especially in this rapidly changing world of technology and medicine. The author has no medical training and is in no way connected to the medical profession. Peter Kray is an experienced reporter and editor who was asked to write this book as a result of his close relationship with someone who spent three decades searching for the answers to a number of potentially lethal personal health problems - problems that often went unsolved at some of the top healthcare facilities around the nation. These problems were eventually solved, often in the most unlikely of places, but always as the result of dogged persistence, asking the right questions and making the right decisions.

To read The Monster all you need is to want to live a healthier life. You need to be able to question how you have viewed your mental and physical health in the past, and to be able to put your present lifestyle up for challenge. You need to have an open mind, or the desire to acquire one, to be able to identify where in your life The Monster may be hiding.

Here's to turning a light on.

the monster

The sound of church bells hung heavy in the air. All over the little town of Perfectville people stopped in their tracks as if a black cloud had suddenly passed in front of the sun.

The birds stopped chirping, the breeze stopped blowing, and on the playground, where the children had been running and laughing, there was only scared silence. As if in a trance, the boys and girls walked slowly to the edge of the blacktop to look through the fence at the little white church across the street where a black hearse was waiting.

They grabbed the metal links in their little fingers and chewed on their little lips as a whisper began to rise amongst them.

"Who is it?" they asked. "Who did The Monster get this time?"

Bobby, a blonde-haired boy with big blue eyes, was so scared and excited he couldn't be still, and he pulled at the fence and bumped against the shoulder of the dark-haired boy beside him.

"What's going on?" he asked Worrie.

But the dark-eyed, sleepy-faced boy was busy trying to fit a fourth piece of gum into his mouth. He had just chomped it down enough to answer when the church doors swung open and the air filled with the sad sound of the church organ.

"Here they come," someone said. The children pressed their noses against the fence as six big men in black suits stepped through the church doors carrying a long redwood coffin between them. As they walked into the light, the lacquered wood of the long red box seemed to burst like fire in the sunshine.

Bobby saw the sharp reflection of the sun and felt as though he'd been struck by lightning. He shivered to think of someone inside the long box. Someone who didn't know the sun was shining. He felt cold, as if his lungs had stopped working.

"Who is it?" he gasped.

"It's Mister Mover," Worrie hissed, frantically chewing his gum.

"The football coach?" Bobby asked, dumb-struck. "But he's the toughest man in town. What happened?"

Worrie looked at Bobby as if he were stupid. "The Monster got him."

"The Monster? But how could he get him?"

Worrie was annoyed. "Because," he said, "The Monster can get anyone."

Mister Mover was the biggest man Bobby had ever seen. His arms were as big as most people's legs. His big shoulders crowded up past his neck into a wave of rippled muscle that rolled right up to the back of his head, and he had such a great big smile that even his teeth looked as if they had muscles.

"Mister Mover's like Superman," Bobby said.

"You mean Mister Mover *was* like Superman," corrected Sika, the red-haired girl beside them. Sika had allergies and wiped her nose whenever she said anything.

"Even Superman can't fight The Monster," she said, and wiped her nose with the tissue in her hand.

Bobby didn't believe anyone could hurt Mister Mover. He watched in shock as the hearse sunk with the weight of the coffin. There was the sound of car doors slamming. The black hearse pulled away from the curb, followed by three black limousines. The black roofs glittered in the light that broke through the trees onto the funeral procession.

Quietly, the children turned back to the playground. All except Bobby, Worrie and Siku, who stared down the street after the limousines.

"Do you believe in The Monster?" Bobby asked suddenly.

"What do you mean?" Worrie said. The question surprised him.

Sika pulled her inhaler out of her dress pocket and took a deep breath. "Everybody says there's a Monster," she said. "There must be one."

"But none of us believe in vampires or ghosts or werewolves. **So why do people believe there is a Monster?**" he asked them.

the reporter

News of the Perfectville Monster eventually reached Big Town. I was a reporter with the Big Town Newspaper, and they sent me to Perfectville to find out what was going on.

In Big Town I had a reputation as a good reporter. People said I wrote stories that didn't pull any punches. They gave me nicknames like "The Grip," "The Big Scoop," and "Mister Deadline." I was the perfect choice to get the story, especially since The Perfectville Monster had become the talk of Big Town. Everywhere you went, from the smoky bars to the greasy spoons and along the smoggy, bustling streets, people were telling stories about a Monster that was "getting" everyone in the tiny, distant town.

Each new story was more unbelievable than the last, about how a ravenous, unstoppable creature was chasing people through the streets of Perfectville, hiding in their closets and waiting under the covers in their bedrooms. And every story had the same ending: The Monster always got its man, or woman.

So I wasn't surprised the day I walked into work and my editor called me into his office and pulled the shades down. He told me what he knew as he handed me a train ticket, then stood up, shook his finger at me and said, "Listen, Grip, if you can't get the story, no one can!"

When I walked out of his office, everyone knew where I was going. They looked at me as if I had been fired. Tim, the sportswriter, shook my hand and said, "Good luck, man."

I could feel their eyes on my back as I grabbed the last donut from the break room and took the elevator down. As a young reporter I used to run the stairs. I didn't have time now, and it had gotten harder with my smoking and the weight I had put on. As I bit into the donut's jelly center and the elevator doors closed, I felt as if I might never see the place again.

On the train I was nervous. I went to the bar for beers and a cheeseburger with blue cheese and bacon, and a side of cheese fries with gravy on them thinking that might calm me down. I felt better with the beer. I began to think what a good story I would write and how people wouldn't be afraid after I explained everything. Monsters didn't exist. Something else was going on.

The train left the city and rolled into the

green countryside as I wondered if the people of Perfectville were exaggerating some local legend. I lit a cigarette and thought about the bogeyman. He seemed real when I was a child - more real because of the strength of my imagination.

As the day faded and the train approached Perfectville, I decided The Monster was probably the result of a whole town's collective imagination gone out of hand. But then I saw the water tower. It changed my opinion. Over the black "Perfectville" lettering, in bright red paint, someone had painted the words, "Monster Town." It looked as if it were painted in blood the way the bottom of the letters had dripped down.

I jotted a note: **People believe in Monsters when there's something they can't control, or don't understand.**

worrie

Bobby and Worrie walked home together. They usually walked with Sika, but she didn't appear after all the other kids had already gone. They decided her allergies had been acting up, or that she had felt sick and left before the bell rang.

"Poor Sika. She gets whatever cold is going around," Bobby said.

Worrie nodded. "Even if there isn't one."

It was hot. They walked without talking as Worrie ate a candy bar then licked the melted chocolate from his hands. Worrie always had candy or a can of Sugar Fizz with him. Bobby didn't eat sugar at home. Sometimes he shared with Worrie, but he hadn't been hungry since he'd seen the coffin.

He looked at the blue sky and rows of leafy green trees and tried to imagine how The Monster might jump from behind a bush or parked car and grab him. The thought of it scared him, and he looked over his shoulder just in case The Monster was watching them. Then he remembered something Worrie said that morning.

"Hey," he said, grabbing Worrie by the shoulder. "How did you know about Mister Mover? How did you know it was The Monster that got him?"

Worrie blinked as if Bobby had woken him. "How did you know The Monster got him?" Bobby asked again, gripping Worrie's shoulder harder.

"Everyone knew The Monster would get him," Worrie said, and shook away from Bobby's grip. "Mister Mover knew it before anyone."

"What?" Bobby's jaw dropped. "Mister Mover knew The Monster would get him?"

"Mister Mover knew it first," Worrie said. "He knew it for a long time. But he thought The Monster would go away. He thought he would have time to change, but he waited too long."

It's always too late in the end, Bobby thought. That was one of his father's favorite sayings. "But how did it happen?" he asked. "I still don't understand."

"He saw The Monster a year ago." Worrie said. "He was sitting in his office after practice and The Monster burst in and said, 'Mister Mover, I'm comin'!' then the pain in his heart began."

"Why didn't he run?"

"He didn't want to miss the football season."

The new season was starting and everyone said the team would be good. Bobby thought of how Mister Mover wouldn't see any of the games. He wondered why Mister Mover hadn't done something. Hadn't just the sight of The Monster scared him?

"What does The Monster look like?" Bobby asked, even though he was afraid of what Worrie would tell him.

"What you're most afraid of," Worrie said. "Like a big shadow that sucks all the light out of the room, or a skeleton in black robes. I think it's a slimy old zombie with warts and cuts that can burp out of the holes in his hands."

"Really?"

"Yep, or even his elbow or his forehead. He can even burp from out of the middle of his back. And because of all the gas inside of him, he burps all the time."

They both laughed nervously. "I bet he could burp out of his ear," Bobby said, and they laughed and made burping sounds.

"But that's not all," Worrie said. "His breath can rot your lungs. And he's got one hundred saws in his mouth to bite you, and one hundred eyeballs on the end of one hundred snakes on his head to watch where you run."

It had been a hard day for Bobby. When Worrie said "snakes," Bobby felt queasy in his stomach, as if he were full of them.

Bobby was afraid of snakes. The mere mention of them made him want to ask Worrie the question that scared him the most. He looked into Worrie's dark, sleepy eyes, and with a trembling voice said, **"How does The Monster get someone?"**

the dark

I got off the train alone at the Perfectville station. There was no one else on the platform. No
conductor. No taxi cabs waiting. As the train blew
its whistle and chugged off down the tracks, I felt
as if the dark had grown around me, as if I were
the only person out that night in "Monster Town."

The station was a red brick building with
vending machines and a pay phone. I decided to
call for a cab. As I picked up my bags something
moved in the wind behind me, startling me. It
was just a newspaper. Then the breeze shifted
and I thought I heard footsteps. My heart raced.
"Hello," I called. "Hello." But there was no one.

I was scaring myself. I hurried inside to make
my call. I also bought two candy bars to help calm
me down. I craved them. My body always craved
candy at some part of the day, or cigarettes, coffee
or a stiff drink. I was always hungry for something.

The dispatcher said a cab was on its way.
"The cab," she said. Only one driver was willing
to work at night. It would take 10 minutes. She

sounded out of breath as she said, "You wait right there. Peggy's coming."

I ate a candy bar and felt better. Then I ate the other one and wanted a cigarette, but there was no ashtray, so I walked outside to smoke.

I was glad to know the cab was coming. I started to relax with the first puff of nicotine, but then my heart stopped at the sound of a loud crash from the other side of the building.

I dropped my cigarette and started to run, but only for a few short steps. Where was I going? I looked around. I felt as if I were a deer in the headlights, sweat on my brow, waiting for the worst to happen.

But nothing happened. There were no more sounds. I decided to find out what was going on. I tiptoed to the corner of the building to take a look, barely touching the brick wall with my fingertips, peeking around the other side as suddenly, I was face to face with it! The Monster! What a hideous, terrible thing!

Whatever it was, we both screamed. Then we both tried to run. And both tripped over our own feet, and fell to the pavement, panting and shaking. Two scared fat men.

"Who are you?!" I gasped, looking at the big man. He was pale and he had a big belly that hung from under a dirty T-shirt. His teeth were yellow and stained. As the blood came back to his face I saw he had a jaundiced color, and his eyes were yellow too, as if something were spoiled or rotten about him.

"I'm the janitor?" he coughed. "Who are you?"

"I'm a reporter," I replied. "I'm here to write a story about The Monster. When I heard that crash I thought you were him."

"The Monster, huh?" he cackled, and coughed. Then he relaxed, reaching into the pocket of his T-shirt for a cigarette. "Well you sure picked the perfect time to find him."

"How's that?" I said, and pulled out a cigarette of my own. I thought I would be sick without one.

"He loves the dark. He likes to sneak up when you can't see him."

I nodded as we lit our cigarettes. "How come you're out then?"

"You kiddin'?" He looked at his big stomach. "I'm not gonna be hard to find. I can't run. Besides, I work in the dark. The Monster works in the dark. It's a match made in heaven."

It gave me goose bumps the way he said it. He had done some hard living. His face was covered with bumps and deep wrinkles. His nose was red and swollen. I wondered if he felt trapped by his body the way I sometimes did. I wondered if he was looking at me the same way and thought I caught a friendly look, but then he coughed on his cigarette and it was gone.

"Couldn't you clean in the daytime?"

"You tellin' me how to do my job?" he said, and stumbled to his feet.

"No." I stood up, too. I was surprised by how angry the question made him. "I thought it would be easier when you could see everything. And you wouldn't have to worry about The Monster coming around."

"He can get me when he wants. Now if you'll excuse me, I've got work to do. I hope you're lucky with what you're trying to find."

I didn't like the way that sounded. I watched him walk away. In my notepad I wrote: **The Monster comes in the dark, when you can't see him.**

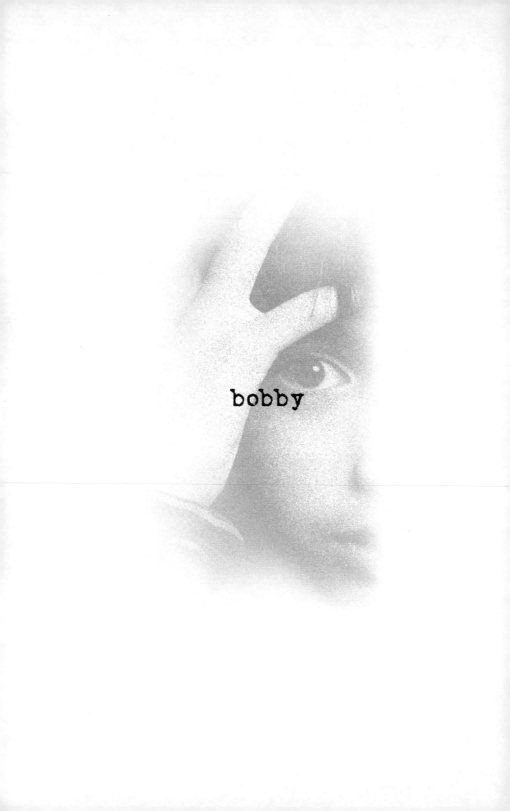

bobby

It was dark when The Monster came to Bobby's room. Everyone was sleeping. Bobby sat bolt upright in bed. Had he heard something?

It sounded like fingernails scratching. He slid up against the wall, clutching his pillow, listening. Scritch, at the window. Scritch. Bobby froze. Scritch. Beads of sweat appeared on his forehead. Scraatch! He dove under the covers, pulling his pillow in after him.

Did The Monster see him? What would it do to him? He tried to make himself as small as possible under the blankets. He remembered what Worrie had said about The Monster having cut glass for hands. Was it cutting the glass? Under the covers, he felt he was drowning.

Craaackk! The glass broke on the floor and the window banged open. There was the creak of a footstep on the floor. Another. Then Bobby heard a snorting, snuffling, gnashing of teeth and stomping of feet, and suddenly, like a string of wet firecrackers, a barrage of burps that seemed to roar from every pore of the mass moving toward him.

The smell was unbearable, a garbage dump in the rain. Even under the covers he couldn't help but gasping. Bobby felt sick. He choked and he coughed. Then he shivered, because now The Monster knew where he was hiding.

Slowly, like a hard cloud of gas, it came toward him. Bobby squirmed under the covers in fear. He felt it reach out to grab him. At the very last, he remembered his secret weapon: "MOM!" he screamed at the top of his lungs. "DAD! HELP! MOOOOM!"

The gas fell away as he screamed. It swept back to the window as lights came on in the house. There were footsteps in the hall. As it left, The Monster's voice boomed as loud as a thunderclap. "Bobby," it growled. "I'm comin'!" He threw up on the floor as his parents ran in.

"Geez, Bobby, it stinks in here," Bobby's dad said. Then he looked where the glass from the window was scattered across the floor. "What're you doing?"

"Honey," Bobby's mother said as she ran toward him. "What happened?"

"It was The Monster," Bobby said.

They looked at each other in terror.

"Mom. Dad," Bobby said. **"What do you do when The Monster comes?"**

peggy

Peggy drove the cab. She was tall, with long silver hair. When she walked up, I felt as though she had come to save me from the railroad station.

"Howdy!" she said, and her brown eyes sparkled. "Welcome to Perfectville."

"Thanks," I said, as she grabbed my bags and tossed them in the trunk. "It's nice to see a friendly face."

I thought she was in her 50's because of her gray hair. She was vibrant and full of life. She had a big smile and a way of walking with her shoulders straight back, like a tree that was moving.

"Where are you going?"

"The hotel. Downtown."

I heard there was only one hotel downtown. She didn't ask again. She reminded me to buckle up, hit the meter and started driving.

"Are you a medicine man?" she asked, grinning.

"A who?"

"I guess not." She looked back at the road and

laughed. "A lot of pill company people have been coming to town."

"Really?" I'd make a note of that after a beer at the hotel. I felt sick from being scared and traveling. Drinking a beer would help me relax again.

"What are you selling?"

"Nothing. I'm a reporter. I'm Monster hunting."

"Well," she laughed again. "You better start with me then."

"How's that?" I leaned forward, thinking she was joking.

It was quiet as she watched the road. Then, at a stoplight, she looked over her shoulder at me with bright brown eyes and said, "Because The Monster spent 25 years trying to get me. But I beat him."

I took out my pen and notebook and wrote the date down.

"What happened?"

"I broke my neck when I was 14, in a sledding accident. There had been a big snowstorm and we went to the big hill near town. I hiked up further than anyone. I was going as fast as a shot when I ran right into a rock on the way down."

"Were you paralyzed?"

"No. But I probably should have been. I don't

know why I wasn't. I don't know why it didn't occur to me that my neck was broken. It was 25 years before I found out what was really wrong."

"How did that happen?"

"The Monster Killers. That's what we call them. They said I was scraped up and just needed some rest at home."

"No X-Rays?"

"Nothing. A week later I went to another Monster Killer because I was in so much pain. He moved my bones around, which wasn't the best thing for what was wrong. The Monster was in my life then. The fight was on."

"The Monster?"

"Yes. The headaches. Sleeplessness. The helpless feeling. The pain."

"But a real Monster?"

"What would you call something that thrives on disease and pain?" Her brown eyes seemed even brighter. "What else do you call something that makes you feel like you've died before you're gone?"

I had no answer. But I saw the fire in her eyes and felt the strength in her voice. As the light turned green, I thought that if The Monster were to jump into the cab right then, we would be fine.

"How did you get better?"

"I turned a light on."

"You turned a light on?"

"It sounds simple now, but for 25 years I searched for simple. All that time, I was trying to shine a light on what was really wrong."

She told me what it took to "turn a light on." In high school, she saw a new Monster Killer every week, but all she ever got were sleeping pills to help her rest from the pain. In college, she took water and Saltines to bed so when the pain woke her up, she had something to wash the pills down. It felt like a nail in the back of her skull. She said she started drinking and taking drugs because she wanted to shut her mind down.

"I didn't want to think. But I knew I had to keep searching. When I was sober, I kept looking for someone to help me. I kept believing that somewhere, someone could tell me what was wrong."

Instead, they put her in a mental hospital. The pain was in her head, they told her. To get out, she pretended to agree with them. Then she got a job as a dental assistant and stole Novocain that she injected into the base of her skull. When she finally found a Monster Killer who would sever her facial nerves, so she wouldn't feel anything, she was losing feeling in her fingers and toes. She was running out of time.

"The pain was all I had. That was The Monster's message. I was going to be paralyzed if I didn't find out what was wrong."

I couldn't believe she was talking about herself. She was so calm, as if watching another road I couldn't see. She seemed to glow when she told me how she found the person who healed her. She said she cried to hear someone tell her they knew what was wrong.

"No one else ever believed I was broken. It was the first time I felt I could start getting better. The first time."

As she pulled up to the hotel I was still writing notes in the back, trying to get it all down.

"It took two years to put everything back in order. Sometimes it was very hard. A lot of times I wanted to quit, but after looking for that long I knew it wasn't an option. I know most people aren't sick like I was. But even if they're a little sick, they should know what's going on. Otherwise, when it really hurts, it may take that much longer to find out what's wrong."

As she drove away, I wrote: **"You search until you turn a light on."**

the monster center

Bobby's parents took him to the Monster Center. It was two in the morning. His dad carried him into the Victim Room where all the Monster Killers were standing around with their white coats on.

"It's my son," Bobby's dad said. "Can you help him?"

The Monster Killers took Bobby from his father's arms and put him in a wheelchair with a blanket over him. They wheeled him down a long hallway. The bright lights and white walls confused him, but he felt much better than he thought he should. In fact he felt pretty good since he threw up, but he had never gotten sick without really being sick before, and The Monster had scared him. He could see his parents were scared, too. He thought something very serious must have happened.

He was wheeled into a room where there was a metal table he was asked to sit on. One of the Monster Killers walked in and Bobby thought he looked very brave and must be the head of the

Monster Killers. He nodded at Bobby's parents as he came in and started to ask them all questions.

"The Monster came in my window," Bobby told him. "He burped on me and made me sick. Then he ran away when my parents came in."

"The window?" the Monster Killer said, and looked very seriously at him.

"He broke the glass with his razor hands and came right in." Bobby told him.

"Are you sure The Monster wasn't hiding in your closet? Or under your bed? He could have been in your dirty laundry bin. We all know how much The Monster loves the dirty laundry bin."

"No," Bobby said. "He came in through the window."

"The glass was broken," Bobby's father said. The Monster Killer stared at him.

"There's just no such thing as The Monster coming in through the window," the Monster Killer said. "A Monster doesn't just break into your house. You have to let The Monster in."

"We wouldn't let The Monster in!" gasped Bobby's mother.

The Monster Killer didn't say anything. He examined Bobby, looking in his ears, shining a light at his eyes. Then he stopped and walked back to a row of shelves that were filled with jars of pills and medicine.

When he walked back, he said, "I only know of three ways to treat him."

"Do any of those ways deal with The Monster coming in the window?" Bobby's mother said, tilting her head back and looking down her nose at him.

"I just don't believe that can happen," he said. "All I can think is that The Monster was hiding in the closet, somehow got locked out, and was trying to find a way back in."

"What are the treatments for that?" Bobby's father asked him.

"Well, there's Monster Pill, there's Monster Powder, or there's Monster Injection," he said. "I'm very comfortable handing out Monsters Pills and Monster Powder, but only in the most extreme cases do I give a Monster Injection."

"What does that do?" Bobby's mother asked.

"Well," the Monster Killer said. "That's for the most extreme cases. Basically, we put another Monster inside of him."

"Well what about the Monster Pill then?" Bobby's father asked.

"That's if The Monster is hiding in the closet," the Monster Killer said. "It slows your body down so the Monster can't detect you. Your breathing and heart rate are reduced so he never senses any life in the room, especially when you're sleeping."

"Isn't that harmful?" Bobby's mother asked.

"You might not want to get off the couch," the Monster Killer said. "Because you're sleeping so slowly, you have to sleep a little longer. But so far, that's the only side effect we've found."

"And the powder?" they asked.

"That's if The Monster is under the bed. Because he always knows when you're in the room, to get to bed you have to walk right past him."

"Right?"

"The powder lays a white chalky mist over the body that feels to The Monster like dead skin. He thinks he already got you, and goes looking for another victim."

"What does that do to you?"

"Well it slows you down," the brave man laughed. "It's not easy walking around in all that heavy, chalky skin."

"That's all you've got?" Bobby's mother said.

"Well," the Monster Killer said, and Bobby could see that he was upset. "I don't think the boy knows what kind of Monster he saw. I think you should strongly consider starting him on a battery of Monster Medicines."

Bobby could see his mother was mad. She said, "I think we should wait and see how he feels in the morning."

"That's the risk you take," the Monster Killer said.

"The risk," Bobby's father said, "would be doing something we can't undo again."

Bobby was confused as they walked out of the Monster Center. He thought the Monster Killers would hand him a pill to take and he would never see The Monster again. Why was he going home without medicine?

"Mom?" he said. **"Why didn't I get any medicine?"**

pep

I ate breakfast in the hotel restaurant. I had eggs Benedict, rolls with butter, a pancake and black coffee to wash it down. I was constipated. I thought a big breakfast would open me up. But I felt even more compacted. So I lit a cigarette and walked around town.

Perfectville was a nice town. The people were well-dressed, bright white awnings shaded the stores, and everything seemed like it had just been cleaned. In fact, I could smell ammonia in the air. It started to smell like someone with a mop bucket was following me around.

It made me nauseous, and I lit another cigarette to settle my stomach. To get away from the smell I started up a side street, walking under a row of elms trees away from town. My feet were tired after a few blocks, and I was glad to find a park with shady trees and a bench where I could sit down.

I listened to the birds and looked at the blue sky. I was thinking how peaceful Perfectville seemed when a dark-haired young woman walked toward me and sat down.

"Hello," I said.

"Hello," she said. "Isn't it a beautiful day?"

"Yes," I said. She was small, with big brown eyes, short dark hair and the happy face of a person who never expects anything to go wrong. "I'm surprised more people aren't out enjoying it."

"People in Perfectville stay inside a lot," she said.

"Maybe it's because of the smell of ammonia," I said sarcastically.

"Oh, that's just their idea of Monster prevention. They think if things are clean they won't get sick, so they constantly wash everything. It's more complicated than that, but it makes them feel good. They just forget to clean themselves inside, too. And they put too much faith in chemicals. I bet you didn't know there are cleansers like ammonia in that cigarette you're smoking."

"No, I didn't," I said, and looked at my cigarette as if I might see them. Then I asked, "What do you mean by Monster prevention?"

"You don't know about The Monster?"

"It's why I came to Perfectville," I said. "I'm a reporter. I'm Monster hunting."

"Really? What are you writing? I could tell you how I met him?"

She told me her name was Pep as I pulled out my notebook.

"What do you know about The Monster, Pep?" I asked, and started writing.

"I know I had four surgeries to try and remove him," she said, and her bright eyes flickered. "They tried to cut him out four times by the time I was 29."

"What happened?"

"It poisoned me. It made me feel like my insides were hardened," she said.

"How old were you when it started?"

"I was 13. But the Monster Killers told me I was too young to have seen him."

"Does The Monster attack many children?"

She looked thoughtful. "I think it was because my body was changing. If The Monster starts young, then people get used to living with pain. Nobody ever told me what to expect from growing up, or how to tell when something was wrong."

"How did you know then?"

"When I couldn't stand up in the morning. That's when knew something was wrong." She smiled and shook her head at the memory. "If it didn't hurt too much for me to stand up, then I was fine."

"Did you get help?"

"I got drugs for the pain. But the pain wasn't the problem. I had to convince them to operate on me to prove that something was really wrong."

She said the Monster Killers had to chisel her apart to remove the poison. Then they cut her open again, and again. She realized the pain wouldn't stop until all her insides were gone.

"The Monster was eating me one little bit at a time."

"What did you do then?"

She called it Star Trek medicine. She said she met someone who could look inside her cells. Someone who found the poison deep inside her, layered under the years, and who slowly pulled it out layer by layer, working back in time.

"Your body is like an onion," Pep said. "Each year was like another layer over the original cause of my pain. Each year, it was deeper in my cells. I had to pull it out a year at a time – all of the poison, and all the pain."

She smiled, a beautiful smile, full of contentment.

"And you know what?" she said. "When it was done, I felt as good as I did before the pain began."

She had started graduate school and was getting married in the spring. She said it was the first time in her life she felt she could make plans.

She smiled as she watched me taking notes. "You have to be a reporter," she said. "Tell your own story. No one can tell that story like you can."

Then she said something else that I wrote down. She said, "My mistake was to go back to people who weren't helping me, and who didn't know what was wrong. **If it doesn't help you, it's not medicine.**

monster medicine

Bobby slept soundly that night. The Monster didn't come back to see him. But just in case, Bobby's father slept in a chair beside him.

In the morning, his mother made him a big breakfast, with juice, water, fruit and oatmeal. Bobby wasn't scared anymore. He was beginning to think it had all been a nightmare. He could hardly wait to tell Worrie and Sika what had happened.

"Mom. Can I go to school when I'm done?"

"I'll take you after lunch. I want you to rest a little more. And just today, I think you should skip gym."

"Oh." Bobby thought lunch would be the best time to sit down and tell his story without interruption. He wondered if he should not feel as good as he did. Was there something his mother wasn't telling him?

"Mom," he said. "Why did The Monster get Mister Mover? Did he do something wrong?"

His mother sat down at the table. "Mister Mover was a very nice man," she said. "He just didn't change his life when The Monster told him to. He didn't listen when The Monster talked to him."

"What did the Monster tell him?"

"Well, I'm sure some of what The Monster said was that Mister Mover needed to take care of the inside of his body as well as he took care of the outside, like someone who didn't take care of his car's engine. He took care how he looked, but he didn't eat things to make him run right. That's why The Monster got him."

"But The Monster talked to me last night?" Bobby said. "What if I didn't listen?"

"Oh honey," she said, and came over and hugged him. "You don't have to be afraid of The Monster. Do you know why?"

Bobby shook his head.

"Because you're so healthy and because we love you so much. And because you're so smart that if The Monster ever came to try and get you, then first he'd have to answer all your questions."

Bobby nodded. He thought he understood. But if The Monster came back, he didn't think that he would want to talk to him.

Later, Bobby's mother let him watch television. There weren't any cartoons on, so he watched a game show. The game wasn't very good though, and the people didn't seem very smart. Bobby thought the commercials were more interesting.

Most of them were commercials for Monster Medicines. Bobby was surprised to see there were so many Monster Pills and Monster Potions, Monster Powders and Monster Lotions, and pills that made you happy when The Monster was in your life by changing your emotions. He wondered how The Monster had time to chase so many people. And why, with so many Monster Medicines available, it got so many of them.

When he went back to school he almost ran down the hall to tell Sika and Worrie about his trip to the Monster Center, but something made him stop. The halls seemed so quiet. Too quiet. When he walked into his classroom he saw why. All of the children had Monster Powder on.

They were covered in white chalk from head to toe, and their eyes were red and blinking. When they coughed, little clouds of powder puffed out. When Bobby walked in they all turned to look, glaring because he wasn't covered in powder like the rest of them.

"Are you okay Bobby?" his teacher asked, obviously concerned. "Would you like to go and see the school nurse to get some Monster Powder on?"

"No thank you," Bobby said. "My mom and dad said I don't need it. I'm fine."

"Really?!"

"I feel fine," Bobby said. Suddenly he wasn't so sure. "May I sit down?"

"Yes, Bobby. Just let me run down to the office to get something," She left the classroom as Bobby made his way to his seat. Everyone was still looking at him. Even Worrie and frail little Sika, who couldn't stop coughing.

"Aren't you afraid of The Monster?" Worrie hissed as Bobby sat down.

"Yes," Bobby said. "Last night he tried to get me. Just like you said he would. I even went to the Monster Center. But I'm fine."

"He came to everyone's house," Worrie said. "That's why everyone has Monster Powder on."

Worrie's lips were purple from Sugar Fizz soda. Bobby thought that the Monster Powder, combined with Worrie's dark, heavy eyes, made him look like a scary clown.

"Why don't you have Monster Powder on?" Sika coughed.

"Because that's for Under the Bed Monster," Bobby said. "The Monster came in through my window."

"Me too," Worrie said.

"Me too," said Sika.

"Then why do you have Monster Powder on?"

"Because," Worrie said.

"Yeah," Sika said. "We had to take something."

"Bobby!" It was the teacher. She had brought the principal with her. They motioned for Bobby to come to the front of the classroom. "Will you come with us? We've called your mother to pick you up. It's best if you're not around the other children until you put the Monster Powder on."

All the other children looked at Bobby. He wondered what he had done wrong. He didn't think Worrie and Sika should have the Monster Powder on. He thought probably a lot of the kids shouldn't have Monster Powder on. He thought it was making Sika sicker, and that made him mad.

"Why are you all taking the wrong medicine?" he said, as the principal came and grabbed him by the sleeve, pulling him from the classroom.

the scoop

In Perfectville, everyone saw The Monster eventually. It always surprised them. Everyone thought The Monster would get someone else. Many people said they didn't believe in Monsters until it happened.

After it happened, they did one of two things. Some of them turned a light on. Their eyes were bright, and they were happy, and they made me feel happy, too, so that I began to think of them as "the Sunshine."

But the others tried to ignore the fact that The Monster had come to see them. They lived in the Shadows. The Monster still haunted them. "That's just the way it is," they said, or "no one can help, I've asked everyone." Their eyes were yellow and sick, and there was a sense of fear about them.

My story was about what divided them. What was it the people in the Sunshine saw? For the people in the Shadows, what was hidden?

At breakfast that morning, by chance, some-one pointed me in the right direction. I had just finished the sausage, bacon, eggs and pancakes I ordered, still trying to open up my insides by sheer mass, and was lighting up a cigarette, when I noticed how the man at the table beside me kept laughing. It was the laugh of a jolly old king, and I turned to ask him why he was so happy this morning.

He laughed and said, "Because it's a beautiful morning."

He had bright red cheeks, bright blue eyes, thin red hair and a ruddy complexion.

"Don't you worry laughing so loudly might attract The Monster?" I joked.

"Actually, I'm scaring him away," he said. "Laughter terrifies him."

"Really? How?"

"The Monster loves the dark. When you laugh, you bring joy into the world. You bring light into a room. Light is hope. Hope threatens him."

"Happy people live longer," he said as I stood up to leave. "There's even research on it. I bet you could find something at the library if you were looking."

He was laughing as I left. I smiled to hear him, and I decided to take his advice. I went to the library. But not for laughter. I wanted information.

When I got there, a blonde-haired man was looking at coffee table books of photographs. He was the only person there besides the librarian. "Hello," he said as I walked past him.

I went to the old newspaper section. The papers were bound in books with the most recent articles on top. As I expected, I found plenty of stories about Monster attacks and Monster sightings. But besides the dates and victims, there was little information. There were no details about what had really happened, nor any Monster descriptions.

The further back, the less information. After 20 years, there was nothing. Not one story. Not one report of anything out of the ordinary, momentous, or even slightly interesting.

I was about to give up when I turned one final page of yellowing paper and suddenly there it was in black and white, the clue that was missing.

"Little Pill Topples Giant Monster," the headline read. There was a picture of six men in business suits and lab coats holding handfuls of pills and smiling. It hit me like a stack of Sunday papers when I saw it. They thought they had killed the thing.

The paper said The Monster would be vanquished by the new medicine. People would never be scared again. No matter how The Monster snuck up, the tiny pill would save them.

"Those were the days, huh?" said a voice behind me. I turned to see it was the blonde man. "When the Magic Pills could cure everything."

"Are you a Monster Killer?"

"Kind of," he said. "But probably not the way you think of one."

"Do you mind if I ask you some questions?"

His name was Pete. He had bright green eyes and a friendly, deliberate way of talking. We sat on the steps of the library while I smoked and asked him questions.

"Not many people in the library," I said.

"I come to look at pictures of art. It's like a mini vacation. People in Perfectville shy away from old things though, even old knowledge. It's too musty for them. They like things that are new and shiny. They think technology and health are the same thing."

"Hasn't The Monster changed things? Things certainly seem different since that story I found, when everyone thought the pills would protect you from him."

"Not so far. It's still eat, drink and be happy because we'll fix you before it's too late. People like to think technology will move fast enough to save them. It's like those allergy ads with blue skies and big yellow flowers, where you take a pill every day and never sneeze again. Nobody mentions how a lot of allergies can be virtually eliminated by diet. Or how once those pills are in you, it's hard to get them out again."

"But if the pills are so bad, why do people use them?"

"Because it's easy. People don't want to have to work to maintain their health. They'd rather find a magic bullet that fixes everything."

"Do the pills help at all?"

"Sure. A lot of them do help, especially if you're sick with infection. But most people shouldn't start there. There's more than one Monster in the world, and there's more than one way to fight him. The best way is with experience and information. The way you live your life is the best medicine."

Then he said something I wrote down.

"When people believe in only one medicine, it's because they've stopped asking questions."

the monster's return

Bobby's mother said it wasn't his fault he had been sent home. Still, he felt as if he were the only kid in the world who hadn't put the Monster Powder on.

The phone started ringing after dinner. It was the other parents. They didn't think Bobby should come back to school until he took the medicine.

"Do you even know what kind of Monster Henry has?" he heard his dad say. "But you still dumped Monster Powder on him, then called me up to tell me how I'm wrong?"

Worrie and Sika's parents called, and Bobby's mother and father talked to them.

"What am I going to do tomorrow?" Bobby asked when they were done.

"I'm going to tell your teacher that no one is going to dump Monster Powder on you," Bobby's dad said. "Then you'll go back to class with your friends."

Bobby wasn't so sure. He lay awake for a long time that night wondering when he would play with Worrie and Sika again. He was still awake after his parents had gone to bed, when the whole town was dark and The Monster came back to see him.

Bobby heard The Monster scratching at the window, and he clutched his pillow, ready to dive under the covers again. He felt the same fear he had the first time, but as he was trying to catch his breath to yell for his dad, a new idea occurred to him. Slowly, he tiptoed toward the sound of the scratching.

Bobby stood at the window for a long time. He couldn't believe what he was doing. Finally, he took a deep breath, counted "1, 2, 3," flipped the latch on the window and in two steps dove back under his covers before it swung open.

Shivering, he wondered if he had done the right thing. He worried about letting The Monster in. But at the first sound of The Monster in his room he realized something had changed. The footstep wasn't as heavy. Then it sounded like The Monster tripped over something. And when The Monster burped, it was barely a squeak. Bobby giggled. He thought The Monster should be embarrassed more than anything.

"That's rude," Bobby said from under the covers.

"Bobby, I'm comin'" The Monster started to bellow, but sputtered out in a coughing fit and finally sat down on the edge of Bobby's bed and said, "why aren't you afraid of me anymore?"

Bobby peeked out from under the covers. He was shocked at the sight of The Monster's 100 eyeballs looking at him. It made him dizzy, and he had to stifle a shiver because of the snakes, but he still gathered up the courage to ask, "Why do you keep coming around?"

"I thought you were sick. I thought all you kids were sick. I figured it would be a good time to try and pick up some business in children."

"Are we sick?"

The Monster rolled all his eyes and gnashed his teeth, then said, "Well, you were sick," he said. "But just because the potato salad was bad on Tuesday. Almost all you little twerps got a little bit of food poisoning."

"But you came through the window."

"Yeah," The Monster sighed, and the saws in his teeth crashed together. "There was a real strong smell blowing in off the landfill, and that seemed to trigger everyone puking. I like to make an entrance. It seemed like good timing."

Bobby sat up straight and asked the Monster, "So what about the Monster Powder?"

"That stuff tastes like chalk!" The Monster exclaimed. "I can't believe it's helping anyone. But it sure slows you down. It makes you easier to get. You little creeps can be pretty quick sometimes."

"So it isn't making them better?"

"Does it look like it's making them better? Boy, I can't wait to see how all those chemicals mix in with your little hearts and lungs. I'm gonna see your friend Sika next. I bet she can't even breathe under that stuff. And that little candy gobbler Worrie will be nearly comatose with his sugar rush gone. That Powder is certainly not helping them!"

It made Bobby mad that The Monster would try to hurt his friends. "Well what is it?" he demanded. "What do you want from us then?!"

"I want to scare you, Bobby. That's what Monsters do. I want you to hide from me and worry about when I'm coming."

The Monster stood up as he talked. "I want you to wake up in a cold sweat in the middle of the night at just the thought of me somewhere in the room," he said, and suddenly he was growing bigger, and burping, so that a stench rose off his body as if a black cloud were filling the room.

"I want you to be afraid to go to the bathroom

in the middle of the night because you think I'm behind the shower curtain," The Monster said, and his voice grew loud and terrible. "I want you to be scared and ignorant of everything!"

He stood up and spread his razor sharp hands and rolled his 100 eyes and gnashed his 1,000 teeth and started up the bed towards Bobby. The trembling little boy backed up against wall. He knew there was nowhere to run. In a second it would be over. But he had one more question.

"What's The Monster afraid of?" Bobby asked as the black stench swept toward him.

the monster killer

I was going over my notes, eating pizza in my room when the pain in my chest began. I couldn't breath and my arms felt numb. I called the front desk and collapsed on the bed, waiting for help to come. It would be too bad if I didn't finish my story. I was so close to finding out how The Monster had gotten everyone.

At the Monster Center they told me it was a severe case of heartburn. I was so happy I barely noticed when the Monster Killer said I was also dehydrated from all the liquor I was drinking, and that I was overweight and should stop smoking.

"It looks like you've got a couple of decisions to make," he told me.

"Decisions?" I just wanted a cigarette to calm down. "What decisions? I thought I was dying and it turns out to be indigestion. Just give me something for the heartburn."

"Don't you realize how you're damaging your heart with the way you're living?"

"Maybe I'm being attacked by The Monster,"

I said, half-joking.

"Without a doubt," he replied, and I noticed his bright green eyes, and that he was casually dressed in a pink oxford and jeans. "I'd say you've been intimate with The Monster for a long time."

That unnerved me. And it made me angry. I thought I would ask him to just give me some pills so I could go back to the hotel room. But then I realized I had yet to ask a Monster Killer any questions.

"So do you really believe in The Monster?" I asked him.

"I believe we are The Monster." He looked me in the eye. "We create him. We invite him into our lives when we don't take care of our health. Of all the relationships in life, the one you have with your health is the one you need to work the hardest at maintaining."

"But I thought your magic pills defeated The Monster. What happened?"

"We were wrong. We thought the knowledge we gained was better than all the knowledge we had, and we over prescribed the magic pills. We had a hammer, so the whole world looked like a nail. We're always learning new rights, and new wrongs."

"Then how do you make decisions?"

"I take an evidence based approach to problems. I use treatments only in the ways they've been studied, and only if they're proven as a successful option."

"But treatments are always being studied," I argued.

"I get the best information I can. But I have to know the numbers before I recommend anything."

"So you're a statistician?"

"I help people help themselves. I tell them what I think I can do for them and what the possible benefits and possible side effects are. My goal is to try to help people be as healthy as I can without doing them harm."

"So why are people looking at so many different options?" I asked. "Aren't you supposed to be the only option?"

"Think about it. A placebo will always have some success against The Monster based solely on the awesome healing power of your mind. That's with no risk. If you eat well and exercise, that rate of success continues to climb. And I've seen everything from prayer to a massage increase the success rate of someone fighting The Monster. I've seen people recover from The Monster attacks just by someone laying their hands on them.

Every victim of The Monster should be willing to pursue his own options. Surgery may be irreversible, and for that reason, should always be a final option."

"But why do the studies always focus on Monster medicine, and not on natural options?"

"It takes a lot of money to study magic pills. You profit when the magic pill is yours, and no one else has another one. Why pay to find out something is effective if you can buy it from anyone."

"So you only prescribe magic pills?"

"I prescribe herbs too, but only if I know the data on them. There are side effects to everything. Some patients take magic pills. Others want herbs. Both have side effects. And in either camp, people don't know enough about what the medicine is doing to them."

"Will the two medicines always be practiced separately?"

"In a perfect world, they'll be practiced together. But I need enough information to tell people what to expect. I have to know I'm not potentially harming someone."

"Don't the pill makers pay you big bucks to push the magic pills for them?"

He laughed. "My generation missed that.

They market straight to the consumer now. These days, people tell me what pills they want me to give them. In most cases, it isn't the treatment I would recommend. Especially with what a lot of those pills can do to your organs. It can be like getting toxic waste out of the ground trying to get them out of your body."

"How do you get The Monster out of your life?"

"By gaining knowledge. From searching and being willing to learn. Good health is good information. Well-being is knowing exactly why you do what you do, and believing it's working. **What scares The Monster most is information.**"

turning the light on

My editor called the next morning. He wanted me back in Big Town. "The vacation's over," he said, "and you better have something good on this Monster thing!"

I broke out in a sweat at the sound of his voice. Despite everything I had in my notes, I still didn't know how it all began. I didn't know how The Monster picked its victims.

Then the phone rang again. It was the parents of a little boy. They wanted to know if I would like to interview him.

"He's talked to The Monster," the boy's father said. "He knows what's happening."

I looked at my watch. If I hurried there was just enough time for an interview before the train left for Big Town.

"I'll be right over," I said. I grabbed a cup of coffee in the lobby and lit a cigarette for breakfast in the cab. At the first sip of coffee I immediately felt pain in my chest again. And then there was a new pain in my gut as if I'd been stabbed, and I doubled over panting and sweating until it was gone. When I got back to Big Town, I would have to find out what was wrong.

The red brick house where we stopped looked like all the other houses in Perfectville. There was a white picket fence, a white door, bright flowers and a green lawn. I gave the cab driver $20 to wait to take me to the train station, then I went to meet the boy who claimed he and The Monster had spoken.

His parents met me at the door. They seemed a little surprised I was so out of breath, and at how hard I was sweating.

"I'm just a little under the weather," I said. "I'll be fine."

They seemed to agree it was okay, and led me into the living room. A blonde-haired boy was running past the windows with an airplane in his hand, flying through the sunshine.

"Bobby," the boy's father said. "This is the man who wants to talk to you about the conversation you had the other evening."

"Okay," Bobby said, and looked at me with bright blue eyes. He set the plane on the table and sat down. The father motioned me to a chair. He said, "We'll be in the next room if you need anything."

I looked at Bobby. He looked healthy and

happy. He watched intently as I wiped the sweat from my brow and wrote his name down.

"My dad said you're looking for The Monster," he said. "Did you find him?"

"I found a lot of people who said they had seen him."

"And you interviewed all of them?"

"Yes. And now I get to interview you. Your parents told me you were the only one in your class who didn't put the Monster Powder on."

"Yep, but now Worrie and Sika won't wear it either. Worrie's not eating candy anymore because he got so fat when he had the Powder on. And Sika's mom got so mad when the powder almost choked her that now she's trying to find a way to get her off all her allergy medicine."

"And what about you, Bobby? What are you doing?"

"I start soccer next week, and Worrie and Sika are going to be on the team, too. And my dad said we're going to go to the beach in the summertime."

"But what about keeping The Monster out of your life?"

Bobby thought for a second. Then he said, "I think that if I keep getting stronger and smarter, then he'll have to try and find a way to catch up all the time."

"But aren't you worried The Monster will hurt you? Isn't that what he told you when you talked to him?"

"The Monster said that it's easier to catch people when they stop living like children. The Monster said it's hard to catch people who are learning and moving around. The Monster prefers when people don't believe in him."

"What happens if you don't believe in him?"

"Then you think that only a miracle will save you. You forget you're fighting a Monster, and stop training."

"Training?" I asked.

"For living," Bobby said.

"How do you do that?"

"By living like you did when you first believed in Monsters," Bobby said. "By eating how you did when your body was still growing, and by walking, running and riding your bike, and by being curious about living."

"But if so many people are in the dark, how does he choose his victims?"

"It's easy. People give themselves to The Monster. When you stop taking care of yourself, you start sending out Monster invitations. Sooner or later, he gets them."

As I was taking notes, the boy started asking me some questions.

"So you've interviewed everyone in Perfectville?" he asked.

"It seems that way. I interviewed a lot of them."

"Do they know why The Monster is coming to get them?"

I thought about that and leafed through my notebook. I remembered the water tower and the note I took. "No," I said. "They don't. They only know that they're afraid of something they don't understand."

"How does The Monster get them?"

I remembered the heavy, sickly janitor who lived alone in the night.

"In the dark," I told Bobby. "He sneaks up on them."

"And what do you do when he comes?"

I thought of Peggy, and how she searched for 25 years for a way to drive The Monster out of her life.

"You turn a light on."

I watched his big blue eyes taking it all in and realized he already knew the answers to the questions he was asking. He just wanted to know if I knew them.

"Why can't the Monster Killer help some-times?

"Because they can't help if they don't have the right medicine."

"Why are people willing to take the wrong medicine?"

"Because they're still in the dark. They stopped asking questions."

"Do you know what The Monster's afraid of?" I thought for a long time about what the Monster Killer had told me when I thought my heart was going to burst open.

"The Monster is afraid of knowledge," I said. "The Monster is afraid of information."

Bobby stood up. I felt as if the lesson were completed. "He hates questions."

"Wait," I said. "What does The Monster look like? No one has given me a description."

Bobby looked at me with his bright blue eyes. Quietly, he said, "I think you've already seen him." Then he went and picked up his airplane.

I thanked the boy's parents. I was still sweating, and felt a little dizzy as I got in the cab. I didn't like what Bobby said about The Monster, how I had already seen him. The Monster Killer told me the same thing. It wasn't until I caught a glimpse of my pasty worried face in the mirror that I realized what they were saying.

"Oh no," I said, and I felt like crying.

"What's that?" the cab driver asked.

"The Monster," I said. "I've seen him."

"Yeah? You better not stay out after dark then."

It was me. The Monster was me. I had created him. I had made him out of booze and cigarettes, chocolate, cheeseburgers and lazy living. And he could be any kind of Monster he wanted with all the doors and windows I had left open.

What scared me more was how long The Monster had been in my life, and how I hadn't done a thing to fight him. Inside my own body, I had only strengthened him.

I panicked as I looked out the window, searching the trees for some sort of answer. My eyes went to the Perfectville water tower that I had seen when I first came to town. The "Monster Town" graffiti was gone. The tower had been repainted and just read, "Perfectville," in big block letters. That gave me hope, and answered my question.

The people in the Shadows, when The Monster comes into their lives, they run and hide and shut their eyes. They say, "I've seen The Monster." But the people in the Sunshine keep looking right at The Monster. They say, "I see him."

I cleared my throat and corrected myself. "I see him."

"What's that?" the cabbie asked, surprised. "You see him?"

"Nothing," I said. "I was just thinking."

I had my story. I had come to Perfectville thinking everyone was running from a fictitious Monster. But The Monster was everywhere. Perfectville was just the first place that was trying to turn a light on.

They were still in the dark in Big Town. My job would be to wake them up. When I got home that night, to my own life, I was going to turn the light on.

backwards

"What do I do next?" That's the question most people ask after reading The Monster. "How do I start improving my health?" or, "If I want to find The Monster in my life, where should I start looking?" If the story of The Monster says anything, it's that there is no simple, one-size-fits-all solution. The Monster is about a process. It's not about answers. It's about waking people up to the idea that they need to be experts on their own health, and they need to start asking questions.

If you want to start improving your health right now, the best place to begin is right where you are sitting. Start by going backwards through your life. When did you feel your health was at its best? Its worst? What's the difference between those two times? Was it where you lived? Who you lived with? What you ate? Where you were working? What's changed since then? You have to understand your own history of physical and mental health for you to understand where you are going.

Often, finding the cause of a problem is the same as finding the solution. For this book to be effective in your life, it needs to incite you to gather information. It needs to empower you into becoming an expert on yourself, and the way your body and mind are feeling. Whether you go to a doctor, an allopathic or complementary healthcare provider, a classroom, the library, or the Internet, you need to pick a subject relevant to your health and start asking questions. You need to choose to take control of your own health and be active in its improvement.

The longer you wait, the longer the shadows grow over The Monster, or the functional illness in your life. The longer you wait for a magic bullet to cure all your ills, the more desperate that search will become. If you start right now, then you've already made progress. So stand up. Go and turn a light on.

Q: Why do people believe there is a Monster?

A: People believe in Monsters when they are afraid of something they don't understand.

Q: How does The Monster get someone?

A: The Monster comes in the dark, where you can't see him.

Q: What do you do when The Monster comes?

A: You search until you turn a light on.

Q: Why am I not getting better?

A: If it's not helping you, it's not medicine.

Q: Why do people take the wrong medicine?

A: When people believe in only one medicine, it's because they've stopped asking questions.

Q: What is The Monster afraid of?

A: Knowledge and information.

When there's a Monster in your room, you turn a light on.

The Monster / Quick Order Form

To order by mail or fax, please send this form with your payment.

QP Distribution
22260 "C" Street
Winfield, KS 67156

Phone: (888) 281-5170 (Toll Free)
Fax: (620) 229-8978
Email: qpdistribution@skyerock.net
Business Hours: M-F 8:00 to 5:00 CST

QTY	Item	Price	Subtotal
1	**The Monster**	**$12.95**	**$12.95**
	KS Residents add 5.9% Sales Tax:		**$0.76**
	Shipping and Handling: (Shipping per book within the USA)		**$4.00**
	Total:		

For multiple book and international orders,
please contact QP Distribution by phone, fax or email.

PAYMENT

☐ **Money Order**
   Make Money Orders Payable to: QP Distribution.

Credit Card: ☐ **VISA**   ☐ **MasterCard**   ☐ **Discover**

Card Number: _____ Expires: _____

Name (as it appears on card): _____

Signature: _____

Shipping Address

Name: _____

Address: _____

City: _____ State: _____ Zip Code: _____

Daytime Telephone: _____ Email: _____